Ollie

Olivier Dunrea

 Houghton Mifflin Company Boston

www.houghtonmifflinbooks.com

The text of this book is set in 20-point Shannon.
The illustrations are ink and watercolor on paper.

Library of Congress Cataloging-in-Publication Data
Dunrea, Olivier.
Ollie / by Olivier Dunrea.
p. cm.
Summary: Ollie is an egg that does not want to hatch until Gossie
and Gertie sit on him and use reverse psychology.
ISBN 0-618-33928-0
[1. Eggs—Fiction. 2. Geese—Fiction.] I. Title.
PZ7.D922 Ol 2003   [E]—dc21   2002151185

Printed in Singapore
TWP 10 9 8 7 6 5 4 3

For Wayne

This is Ollie.

Ollie is waiting.

He won't come out.

Gossie and Gertie have been waiting
for weeks for Ollie to come out.

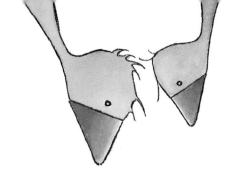

"I won't come out," says Ollie.

He rolls to the left.

He rolls to the right.

He stands on his head.

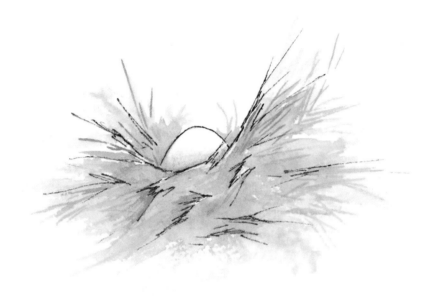

He hides in the straw.
He won't come out.

Gossie pokes Ollie with her bill.

Gertie listens to Ollie with her ear.

"I won't come out!" says Ollie.

He holds his breath.

He rolls out of the nest.

He rolls over the stones.

He rolls under the sheep.
He won't come out.

Gossie runs after Ollie.

Gertie runs after Ollie.

"I won't come out!" says Ollie.

Gossie and Gertie sit on top of Ollie.

"Don't come out," says Gossie.

"Don't come out," says Gertie.

Ollie waits.

Then he begins cracking!

"I'm out!" he says.